Detective Derby Private Eye And The Mystery Of Lighthouse Island

Detective Derby Private Eye, Volume 2

Isaiah Fransen

Published by Isaiah Fransen, 2024.

While every precaution has been taken in the preparation of this book, the publisher assumes no responsibility for errors or omissions, or for damages resulting from the use of the information contained herein.

DETECTIVE DERBY PRIVATE EYE AND THE MYSTERY OF LIGHTHOUSE ISLAND

First edition. September 24, 2024.

Copyright © 2024 Isaiah Fransen.

ISBN: 979-8227155221

Written by Isaiah Fransen.

Table of Contents

Prologue | The Treasure 1
Chapter 1 | Getting Ready To Leave 3
Chapter 2 | Getting To The Cruise Ship 7
Chapter 3 | Getting To Know Each Other 11
Chapter 4 | Arcade Dinner And Much More 15
Chapter 5 | Overboard 19
Chapter 6 | The Mysterious Figure 23
Chapter 7 | The Island Cave 27
Chapter 8 | X Marks The Spot 31
Chapter 9 | The Sad Truth 35
Chapter 10 | Rescue From The Cave 39
Chapter 11 | Saying Goodbye 43
Chapter 12 | Getting To The Airport And Heading Home 47
Chapter 13 | Confronting The Archaeologist 51
Epilogue | The Presentation 55

Dedication "Book Cover Design by ebooklaunch.com"

Prologue
The Treasure

A LONG LONG TIME AGO, there were pirates who sailed the seas hunting for treasure. One day, the pirates spotted a ship and decided that they were going to raid the ship as they had heard it had valuable treasure on it. The pirates headed towards the ship and attacked the sailors! Then they stole all their treasure. The pirates were celebrating and were really happy. The pirates were going through the items that they stole when they noticed that one of the items looked very valuable. The valuable item was a diamond that belonged to a King and Queen far away. The pirates made the decision to hide the valuable diamond so no one could steal it from them. The pirates made the long journey to an island where they found a cave. They went deep into the cave to hide the diamond. Next, the pirates made and set a bunch of traps to stop people from stealing their diamond. Many years have passed since pirates hid the treasure. Since then, no one has been able to find it. However, one archaeologist thought that she had found the hidden treasure. However, when she did a speech at the museum, people quickly noticed that it was a fake. The people laughed at the archaeologist because the treasure wasn't real. The archaeologist stormed out of the museum and was never to be seen again. Well, what happens next, let's find out!

Chapter 1
Getting Ready To Leave

DERBY AND HER PARENTS were getting ready to leave for their cruise. Derby had one last bag to put into the car before heading off to the airport. Scarlett, her mom, yelled at Derby, "Hurry up, we need to go now!" Derby yelled, "I am coming!" Derby went running down the stairs and put her last pieces of luggage into the car. Derby's dad James asked, "Are you both ready to go?" Scarlett and Derby said, "We are ready!" James said, "Okay, here we go!" and they all headed to the airport. Once they got to the airport, they grabbed their bags and headed into the airport to check in and go through security. Derby's parents made it through security, however, Derby was nowhere to be seen! James and Scarlett were wondering where Derby could have gone and asked a nearby security guard if they had seen her. The security told James and Scraellet that they hadn't seen her but that they would keep an eye out for her. Meanwhile, Derby was wandering around the airport and had been distracted by some of the stores. Suddenly, her parents were nowhere to be seen! Derby was wondering where her parents were. She decided to return back to the check in lady to ask if she had seen her parents. The check in lady told Derby, "I think your mom and dad have already gone through security."Derby thanked the check in lady for helping. Derby went through the security gate and was told by the security guard that her parents had gone through security and were looking for her. The security guard checked Derby's carry-on bag before letting her through and discovered her detective collection. The security guard was surprised to see the detective items. They included a magnifying glass, flashlight, detective hat, and a notepad with detailed notes. He said, "You have an interesting collection of detective items. What are your plans?" Derby said, "I wanted to bring my detective stuff just in case I needed to solve a mystery on the cruise ship." The security guard giggled and said, "There shouldn't be any mysteries for you to investigate. You're too young to be a detective." Derby replied, "One time there was a missing bracelet that was stolen, and I helped solve the mystery." The security guard was in shock and let Derby through the gates. Just then, Derby's parents, Scarlett and James saw Derby and gave her a big hug. Then James said to the security guard, "Everything that Derby said is true! Let me tell you, it was a heck of a fiasco!" After getting through security, Derby and her parents headed onto the plane and got into their seats. This was the first time that Derby had been on a plane so she was a bit nervous. James and Scarlett told Derby not to worry and that she would be fine. The flight attendant came over to Derby and introduced herself as Jennifer. She asked Derby if she would like a drink or cookies? Derby said, "Yes please!" Then Derby heard the pilot on the intercom say, "Hello everyone, I am your captain and my name is Mark. We are about to take off so please make sure that you are buckled in!" Derby was getting nervous when the plane's engines started making a lot of noise! The plane moved towards the runway, and picked up speed in preparation of take off! That made Derby even more nervous! The plane safely made it off the ground and took off towards their destination. After being in the air for a couple of hours, Derby looked out the window and saw that they were about to land. Derby was stunned to see palm trees and a large city situated by the water. Mark the pilot spoke over the intercom again and said, "We're about to land at our destination, please ensure that your seatbelts are tightened as we prepare to land." Then the plane touched down on the runaway and safely came to a stop.

Chapter 2
Getting To The Cruise Ship

DERBY AND HER PARENTS got off the plane and headed inside the airport, towards the luggage conveyor belt to grab their luggage. However, Derby was fascinated with the conveyor belt and tried to get onto it! Just as Derby was about to go for a "ride", her parents stopped her and said, "This is not a ride, this is for the luggage!" Derby apologized to her parents and said "I didn't understand what the conveyor belt was for." Derby and her parents gathered their luggage and went outside to call a taxi. The taxi driver arrived and introduced himself as Jordan. Jordan loaded Derby's family's luggage into the trunk of the taxi and then everyone got inside. Jordan the taxi driver asked Derby's parents, "Where are we headed to?" Derby's dad James said, "We need to get to the docks for a cruise ship." Jordan the taxi driver said, "You got it!" He then headed to the cruise ship docks. While Jordan was driving, Derby was looking out the window and noticed that everything was so different compared to Springshore Heights. Derby's mom, Scarlett, said, "I know everything looks so different, but you're going to have such a fun time." Derby and her family finally arrived at the cruise ship dock. Jordan the taxi driver said to James, "That will be $20 for the ride." James thanked Jordan, and gave him the $20 to cover the ride. Next, Debry and her parents headed towards the cruise ship. They presented their tickets to the cruise ship attendant. Derby could hear the captain of the cruise ship announcing,"All aboard!" as they were heading up the ramp onto the ship. Once Derby and her family got onto the cruise ship, the captain of the cruise ship said, "My name is Gary, welcome aboard! I'll get one of the cruise ship attendants to show you to your cabin." Then one of the cruise ship attendants introduced herself and said ,"My name is Lilly, and I will be showing you to your cabin!" So Derby and her parents followed Lilly to their cabin. When Lilly opened the door to their cabin, Derby was shocked and said, "Wow this is really cool!" Lilly gave Derby and her parents the directory that listed all the different things that they could do while on the cruise ship. Lilly left,and Derby and her family reviewed the directory and decided what they were going to explore on the cruise ship. While looking through the directory they saw that there was a shopping mall, arcade and restaurants. Derby was really excited to check some of the places out! Just then, Derby and her parents heard the captain of the ship say over the intercom, "We are about to set sail, please enjoy the ride!" Derby and her family headed to their balcony to watch the ship departing the dock. Derby was really excited because this was her first time being on a cruise! Derby and her parents decided to check out the mall, so they left their cabin and headed down the elevator. Derby and her parents got to the bottom floor where there was a huge mall that went from one end of the ship to the other. Derby was amazed to see so many people and so many places to shop, as well as places to eat. While shopping at the mall Derby accidentally bumped into someone her age and decided to strike up a conversation with them. Derby asked the boy, "What is your name?" The boy said, "My name is Peter, what's your name?" Derby told Peter, "My name is Derby, nice to meet you!" Then Peter's friend appeared and introduced himself to Derby, and said, "My name is Bryan, and I'm Peter's friend." James and Scarlett saw that Derby was making friends and decided to go over and say hello. At the same time, Peter and Bryan's parents noticed that their boys were making friends and headed over to introduce themselves as well. James and Scarlett introduced themselves as Derby's parents. Then Peter's parents introduced themselves as Janice and Carl. Then Bryan's parents introduced themselves as Judy and Bradley. Everyone got along very well! The parents decided to give each of their kids money to get pizza at the pizza restaurant, while they grabbed a coffee at the coffee shop.

Chapter 3
Getting To Know Each Other

DERBY, BRYAN AND PETER headed to the pizza restaurant on the ship, and went directly to the counter. The pizza maker introduced himself as Blake, and asked, "What kind of pizza would you like to order?" Derby asked Blake the pizza maker for a cheese pizza, while Bryan ordered a pineapple pizza and Peter got a pepperoni pizza. Derby and her friends gave Blake the pizza maker money to pay for the pizza, and Blake said "Your order will be right up!" While waiting for their pizza, Derby and her friends sat down at a table to get to know one another. Peter and Bryan asked Derby what she liked to do for fun? Derby told the boys that she liked solving mysteries, and that she recently solved a case about a missing bracelet. Peter and Bryan were stunned and asked Derby how old she was? Derby said that she was nine. Then Derby asked Peter and Bryan what they liked to do for fun? Peter said that he enjoyed playing basketball while Bryan liked watching movies and playing video games. Just then, Blake the pizza maker came over with their pizza and said, "Your pizza is served". Meanwhile, the kids' parents were at the coffee shop on the ship getting to know one another. The coffee shop attendant introduced herself as Kate and asked what kind of coffee everyone would like to order? They all ordered the same coffee. Peter's parents, Janice and Carl, asked Derby's parents, Scarlett and James, about their life back home at Springshore Heights. Scarlett told Janice and Carl that she had recently got out of jail because she was framed by a thief who stole a valuable bracelet from Derby's friend's mom. Scarlett went on to say that the thief planted a fake bracelet in her house which led to her arrest, but that her daughter and her friend from school caught the real thief. James said, "My daughter Derby is a brave girl!". Everyone at the table was shocked and said, "No wonder you needed a vacation!" Janice and Carl told them, "Our son Peter really likes basketball and is an inspiring basketball player!" Judy and Bradley said, "Our son Bryan loves to play videogames and sometimes it's a struggle to get him away from the screen!" Back at the pizza restaurant, the kids had just finished eating their pizza. Peter suggested going to the main deck of the ship to see what was going on up there. Derby and Bryan said, "Sure!" So, Derby and her friends took the elevator to the main deck. They saw that kids could make their own ice cream cones for free! Derby and her friends decided to go and get some ice cream from the ice cream machine. Derby went first. However,when she tried to fill her ice cream cone, the ice cream came out super fast and her ice cream cone almost fell over! Peter and Bryan tried helping Derby to stop the ice cream from falling over and making a mess on the main deck of the ship! However, it was too late and the ice cream was all over the deck creating a sticky mess! The cranky janitor saw what happened and came over to Derby and the kids and said, "Who do you think you are, making this mess? Don't you know how to use an ice cream machine?" Derby apologized and said, "I am so sorry, we're just kids! It's just a bit of ice cream. There's no need to be so cranky!" The janitor said, "Well next time you kids make a mess, you're responsible for cleaning it up!" Bryan suggested that they go to the arcade next, to get away from the cranky janitor! Derby and Peter liked his idea. So, Derby and her friends headed back to the elevator and down to the lower floor of the ship where the arcade was.

Chapter 4
Arcade Dinner And Much More

DERBY AND HER FRIENDS arrived at the arcade and were greeted by the arcade staff who introduced herself as Jane. Jane grabbed Derby and her friends some tokens to play the arcade games. Peter saw a racing car game and challenged Derby and Bryan to a race. Not surprisingly, Bryan won the videogame. Then Peter saw a basketball game and said, "I am going to play that one next". Meanwhile Derby and Bryan played air hockey. Peter managed to get a high score on the basketball game while Derby beat Bryan at air hockey. Then Derby said to Byran and Peter "We had better get back to our cabins, as our parents will be waiting for us." So Derby and her friends headed back to their cabins. Derby arrived back at her cabin and was greeted by Scarlett and James. Derby's parents asked Derby how her time was with Peter and Bryan. Derby told her parents that she had a really awesome time with her new friends, and that they got ice cream and played arcade games. Just then, Derby and her parents heard a knock at the cabin door. It was Peter and Bryan's parents. Peter and Bryan's parents asked James and Scarlett if they would like to have dinner with them in the dining room at the front of the ship. Scarlet, James, and Derby said, "Yes, we would love to!" So they all headed to the dining room for dinner. The group were seated at a big table together, and soon after, a server came and introduced herself as Molly. Molly asked everyone what they would like to order. Derby, Bryan, and Peter ordered fish and chips for dinner. Their parents ordered steak dinners. While waiting for their food to arrive, the group discussed their plans for the next day. Their plans included going for brunch, skating at the ice rink, swimming at the pool, and then going to a live performance in the theater later that evening. Molly came with their food and said "Your dinner is served. I hope you enjoy your food!" The group enjoyed their dinner and had a super fun time talking and laughing. After finishing dinner, the group all headed back to their cabins and went to bed. The next morning, they met for brunch at the dining room. They were all really tired from yesterday and slept in a little later than they had intended. When the group arrived at the dining room, the kids ordered a big stack of pancakes, while their parents decided to have eggs on toast. After finishing brunch, Derby and her friends headed to the skating rink and rented skates and helmets. The boys were the first to get on the ice because they had a lot of experience. However, it was Derby's first time skating. She was falling a lot, and needed to hold onto the boards of the skating rink. Peter and Bryan noticed that Derby was scared and asked her if she needed a hand. Derby said, "Yes please, this is my first time skating and I am not very good yet." Peter and Bryan decided to help Derby get back to the entrance of the skating rink and off the ice. After returning

DETECTIVE DERBY PRIVATE EYE AND THE MYSTERY OF LIGHTHOUSE ISLAND

their skates and helmets. Derby and her friends decided to go for pizza and ordered the same pizzas as before. After Derby and her friends finished their pizza, they headed to the swimming pool located at the top of the ship. Once Derby and her friends arrived at the swimming pool, Peter and Bryan jumped into the pool right away. However, Derby was a bit nervous to jump into the swimming pool! She told the lifeguard that she was afraid of jumping in. The lifeguard reassured Derby and said, "My name is Christopher, don't worry, I will be here to make sure nothing happens so you can have fun." Derby was feeling more comfortable and bravely jumped into the swimming pool and they all had a fun time together.

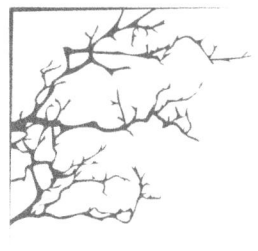

Chapter 5
Overboard

DERBY AND HER FRIENDS got out of the swimming pool and headed to meet their parents at the theater. They arrived at the theater and met their parents outside. They then headed inside to watch the performance. The announcer walked onto the stage and said, "Welcome to our performance, we are so happy to have you here on the cruise!" The announcer went on to say, "Tonight we have a special treat for you! It is a musical performance!" Halfway through the musical performance, the announcer told the audience that there would be a short intermission. Derby, Peter and Bryan decided to take a break and head outside. Then one of the boys noticed a nice smell coming from outside. So, Derby and her friends headed outside to investigate. Normally they don't serve food outside on the ship's deck. That's when Derby and her friends saw a bunch of food in a lifeboat . Derby was very suspicious as to why there would be food in the lifeboat. However, both of the boys jumped into the lifeboat! Derby said, "I don't think you should be in the lifeboat! Something doesn't feel right!" The boys said, "Don't worry, everything will be fine." Derby said "Well okay, I guess I'll join the two of you in the lifeboat!" Derby hopped in. All of a sudden, a man came up to the lifeboat and said, "Ha ha! I've got you!" Then he quickly cut the ropes holding the lifeboat! Derby yelled out, "Oh no!" Then the lifeboat fell from the ship and got washed away from the ship, out into the ocean! Meanwhile, their parents were wondering what was taking Derby and the boys so long to return to the show? They decided to go look for the kids. When the parents got outside of the theater they could hear screaming! Once on the ship deck they saw Derby and the boys on the lifeboat heading out to sea! Derby and the boy's parents were hysterical and yelled, "We need to get to the captain!" They ran to the captain's control room and banged on the door to get his attention! The captain yelled through the door, "This is a restricted area!" The parents yelled back, "This is an emergency! Our kids have somehow gotten out on a lifeboat!" Captain Gary swung open the door! He used his binoculars and saw the kids on the lifeboat! Captain Gary called a rescue team and told them that a group of kids had gotten onto a lifeboat and were drifting out to sea! The rescue team said, "We will have to wait till the morning! It is too dark, and the weather is too harsh to safely search for them!" The next morning, Derby and her friends saw an island. They were heading right towards it. Derby yelled to the boys, "Hold on everyone!" Just before they crashed onto the beach destroying the boat! Peter asked, "Where are we?" Derby said, "I don't know, but I can see a lighthouse in the distance! Maybe we should head there!" So, Derby and her friends headed towards the lighthouse and knocked on the door. Suddenly, the door opened and a man asked, "What brings you kids onto this abandoned island? I've been stuck here for over 50 years and I haven't seen a single person in all that time!" Derby explained that they were on a cruise ship and were tricked into a lifeboat. Then a man cut the ropes of the lifeboat, dropping it into the sea! Then they crashed onto the beach on this island! Derby went on to say that they had no way to get back to the cruise ship. "Our parents are probably very worried about us!" The lighthouse keeper said "My name is Owen. I would like to help, but unfortunately, my communication system is broken. That's why I have been stuck on the island for so long. I am missing some of my batteries to run my equipment. However, you are welcome to stay in the lighthouse." Then Derby said, "Maybe there is something in the lifeboat that we could use to fix the equipment! We will go there now!". Owen the lighthouse keeper said, "Sounds good! I will work on the equipment while you kids are gone! Good luck!".

Chapter 6
The Mysterious Figure

DERBY AND HER FRIENDS arrived at the lifeboat crash site. Derby looked inside the wrecked lifeboat and found a flashlight. She opened up the flashlight and took out the batteries. After retrieving the batteries, Derby and her friends started walking back to the lighthouse. Suddenly, Peter noticed what appeared to be a mysterious figure in the bushes! Peter quickly told Derby that he saw a mysterious figure, but that he wasn't able to get a good look at them. Peter went on to say that the mysterious figure looked like the same person who cut the ropes of the lifeboat. Derby said to Peter, "That's impossible, there's no way he could have gotten onto the island! However, I do think something strange is going on!" Peter said, "You're right! There's no way he could have gotten onto the island." Derby and her friends continued on their walk back to the lighthouse. They arrived at the lighthouse and knocked on the door. Owen the lighthouse keeper answered the door and asked, "Have you found batteries?" Derby said, "Yes we have!" Then Owen the lighthouse keeper said, "It will take me a few days to get the equipment going again. In the meantime, why don't you kids go and explore the island as there are lots of things to see." Derby was in agreement and said, "Yes we will do that!" Then Derby and her friends headed out to explore the island. While exploring the island, Derby and her friends saw someone in the distance. Derby said to her friends, "That's impossible, there shouldn't be anyone on the island besides us and the lighthouse keeper!" So Derby and her friends decided to walk over and talk to her. At the same time, the person saw Derby and her friends coming towards her. Derby asked the person, "Who are you?" She said, "My name is Kaitlyn and I am an archaeologist. I am looking for a long lost treasure on the island." Derby asked Kaitlyn if she had any way to call for help. Kaitlyn the archaeologist said that she had no way of communicating with the outside world. However, Kaitlyn told Derby and her friends that there will be a helicopter picking her up from the island in a couple of days. Kaitlyn the archaeologist said to Derby and her friends, "You're welcome to take a ride back with me on my helicopter if you can help me find the treasure." Derby and her friends said all together, "You have a deal!" In the meantime, the rescue team arrived at the cruise ship and were greeted by the parents and the captain. The parents told the rescue team, "Somehow our kids drifted out to sea in a lifeboat and we have no way to locate them!" The rescue team told the parents not to worry that they would find them. Then Derby's mom Scarlett said, "We are going to come along with you and join the search party!" The rescue team was hesitant and said, "Are you sure that you want to come along with us? It can be very dangerous!" Then Derby's dad James said to the rescue team, "We are coming along. We understand the risks." So, the parents got onto a rescue boat with the rescue team and headed off to sea. The rescue team captain said to the parents, "The weather was bad last night, which may make it hard to locate your kids. However, the kids could have drifted onto an island. Unfortunately we don't know which island they could have drifted to!" The parents started to panic, and said, "Who knows what's lurking on those islands! We hope that the kids are alright!" Meanwhile back at the island, the archaeologist as well as Derby and her friends were deep in the forest looking for clues to find the treasure. Out of nowhere, Peter saw someone in the bushes following them! Peter went directly to Derby and said, "I saw someone in the bushes again!" However, when Peter and Derby looked back the person was gone! Derby and her friends asked Kaitlyn the archaeologist, "Are you sure there is no one on this island? This is the second time Peter saw someone lurking in the bushes!" Kaitlyn confidently said, "No, I don't think anyone else is here." Then, everyone continued to look for clues to the treasure.

Chapter 7
The Island Cave

BACK AT THE LIGHTHOUSE, Owen the lighthouse keeper managed to fix the equipment and radioed for help. Meanwhile, the rescue team was still searching for the kids. Suddenly, they picked up a faint radio signal! The signal was very weak but they were able to trace where the signal was coming from. They heard someone say that there were three kids stranded on lighthouse island! The kids' parents were excited and hopeful that everyone was alright! Derby's mom Scarlett said, "What are we waiting for? Let's head to lighthouse island!" In the meantime, Derby and her friends, as well as the archaeologist, found a cave that was partially submerged under water. Derby and the group were wondering how they were going to explore the cave. Derby said to Kaitlyn the archaeologist, "We have a lifeboat but it crashed on shore." Kaitlyn said, "I have a patch in my backpack, we can use it to fix the lifeboat." So, Derby and the group headed back into the forest to retrieve the lifeboat. Once they arrived at the crash site they decided to carry the boat back through the forest before patching it up. Together they managed to fix the lifeboat and everyone was celebrating. Derby and the group hopped into the lifeboat and headed inside the partially submerged cave. While inside the cave, they noticed that there were spikes coming up through the water. Derby told the group to be very careful because the spikes could pop the lifeboat! Kaitlyn the archeologist told the kids that they needed to get past the spikes to the other end of the cave. So, Derby and the group rowed as carefully as they could past the spikes and towards a dry landing. When Derby and the group got close to the dry landing, they stopped rowing and got out of the boat. Derby said to the archaeologist, "I feel like this cave may have traps!" Before Derby was able to finish her sentence, the archaeologist interrupted her and said, "That's ridiculous! There are no traps in this cave!" Kaitlyn the archaeologist walked further into the cave and suddenly fell into a pit that was disguised as a place that she could walk. Kaitlyn ended up falling into a deep pit and yelled to Derby and her friends, "Help me!" Derby remarked, "I told you that there were likely traps in this cave!" Kaitlyn said, "Get me out of here!". So, Derby and her friends headed back to the lifeboat to get a rope to free the archaeologist from the pit. Derby rolled the rope down to the archaeologist! The rope was just long enough to reach her! The archaeologist grabbed the rope and then the three of them pulled on the rope all at once. Eventually, Derby and her friends managed to get Kaitlyn the archaeologist out of the pit. The kids were almost out of breath. Derby told the archaeologist, "You should have listened to me about the traps! We need to be more careful in this cave!" Kaitlyn the archaeologist weirdly grinned and said, "Fine, you're right." Then Bryan whispered to Derby, "Something doesn't feel right about this. I think we need to be very careful!" Derby reassured Bryan and said, "I'm sure everything will be fine." But deep inside, Derby was also feeling a little bit concerned about the situation, but she wanted to keep her friends calm. Kaitlyn the archaeologist turned on her flashlight to light the way before heading deeper into the cave. Eventually, Derby and the group found themselves at the bottom of a long steep pathway. Out of nowhere, Peter's foot got caught in a rope which triggered a trap releasing rolling barrels! Derby noticed the rolling barrels coming down the steep pathway towards them and yelled, "Ohh no! What are we going to do! We have to free Peter from the rope and then get out of here!"

Chapter 8
X Marks The Spot

DERBY AND THE REST of the group quickly untied the rope from Peter's foot and ran away from the rolling barrels! Derby and the group continued to run down the step pathway away from the rolling barrels! Once they escaped and caught their breath, Derby said to the archaeologist, "That was too close for comfort! We could have been flattened!" Kaitlyn the archaeologist said, "Your friend is the one that triggered the trap this time, not me!" So, the group continued walking deeper and deeper into the deep cave. Then they saw a narrow hallway with a door that had a X on it. Kaitlyn the archaeologist was excited to see the X on the door and said, "Finally, we're almost to the treasure!" Derby reminded Kaitlyn the archaeologist to be careful as there might be more traps! Suddenly, Kaitlyn the archeologist started running towards the door and yelling, "Don't be ridiculous! There's no more traps!" Not surprisingly, Kaitlyn the archaeologist stepped on a tile with a pirate flag on it which ended up triggering another trap! This time the trap was more dangerous than ever! There were cannonballs firing from either side of the hallway! Kaitlyn the archaeologist cried out, "Get me out of here!" Derby and her friends ran towards Kaitlyn the archeologist and instructed her to get down and start crawling towards the door! Derby and her friends were not far behind Kaitlyn the archaeologist. Eventually, Derby and the group managed to escape the trap. Derby realized that she needed to also solve a puzzle in order to open the door. Derby noticed three different levers, and a plaque that read, You must choose the right lever to open the door! If you choose the wrong lever, you will instantly trigger more traps that you must escape from! Derby noticed that there were different symbols on each of the levers. One was an X just like what was on the door. The second lever had a pirate hat symbol and the last lever had a sword symbol. Derby was hesitant to pick the lever with the X because it felt too obvious! Derby's friends came over to help her choose the right lever. Peter agreed with Derby and said, "The lever with the X on seems a little too easy! Maybe you should try one of the other two levers!" Then Byran said to Derby and Peter, "Don't be silly! It's obviously the lever with the X on it!" Then Bryan jumped ahead and pulled the lever with the X on it! Derby and Peter yelled out, "Noooo!" Just then the door opened up, and no traps were triggered! After choosing the right lever, Kaityln the archaeologist ran inside and enthusiastically said, "Finally, I have found the treasure!" Debry and her friends were annoyed and asked, "You mean we found the treasure! Right?" Derby and her friends noticed a huge diamond on a table with a spotlight on it coming from a hole in the top of the cave! Suddenly, Derby and her friends saw a helicopter blocking the spotlight and a rope ladder being dropped down! Derby realized that the person flying the helicopter was the same person who tricked them and cut the ropes securing the lifeboat to the cruise ship! The person flying the helicopter yelled down to Kaitlyn the archaeologist, "It's time to go!" Kaitlyn the archaeologist grabbed the diamond and yelled, "I have the diamond, it's time to pull me up Sayer!" Derby and her friends were confused and said "What about us? We helped you find the treasure!" Kaitlyn the archaeologist said, "Ohh yes, I almost forgot!" Then she proceeded to throw a net on top of Derby and her friends, trapping them in the cave.! Derby and her friends screamed, "What is the meaning of this! I thought we had a deal!?"

Chapter 9
The Sad Truth

BEFORE KAITLYN THE archaeologist left the cave she decided to tell Derby and her friends what led up to this moment. Kaitlyn explained, "I was once a renowned archeologist, known for discovering a famous bracelet now kept in the Springshore Heights museum." Kaitlyn went on to say, "I found another treasure which I thought was real, so I decided to take it to the Springshore Heights museum to be put on display. After bringing it to the museum, I made a speech about it. However, once experts examined the treasure, it turned out to be a fake. The experts laughed at me and I became the laughingstock of the scientific community. I was eventually fired from the museum! So I decided to run away from Springshore Heights and never to be seen there again!" Kaitlyn told Derby and her friends, "One day I was watching the news and saw that you had recovered the stolen bracelet. So,I had an idea and devised a plan to get you onto lighthouse island where I was doing secret archaeologists work. I was able to find out that you were going on a cruise near lighthouse island. That gave me the idea to get my assistant to lure you and your friends onto the lifeboat and cut the ropes causing you to fall into the ocean and crash onto Lighthouse island. Once you and your friends were on the island, I needed to lie to you and your friends about having no communication with the outside world so that I could get help with finding the treasure. Now, with the diamond, I can redeem myself within the scientific community. Unfortunately I must leave you here to prevent you from telling the world what I did!" Derby and her friends said to Kaitlyn, "So this whole thing was a setup? You won't get away with this!"Kaitlyn said, "Too late! I already have! There is nothing you can do to stop me!" After Kaitlyn finished telling Derby and her friends her story, Kaitlyn told Sayer, "Bring me up and into the helicopter!" Kaitlyn and Sayer took off into the sky leaving Derby and her friends behind! Bryan said to Derby, "we have to get out of here!" However, Derby didn't know how they were going to get out of the net and escape the cave. Derby said to Peter and Byran, "We all have to try to push the net off of us together!" Peter and Bryan were in agreement and said, "one... two... three," and all together they pushed the net off of them! Now that they got the net off of them, they needed to find a way out of the cave! The walls were too smooth to climb up and out of the cave. Then Derby and her friends had the idea. They would stand on the table that had the diamond on it, and then climb on each other's shoulders to get to the opening of the cave. Unfortunately, the opening to the cave was too high up and their plan wouldn't work! Then Derby said, "it's no use, we're stuck in here!" Then suddenly, Derby and her friends heard someone calling their names! It sounded like their parents! Derby and her friends started yelling, "We're down here! Help, help!" The voices started getting closer and closer to the opening of the cave. It turned out to be their parents along with the rescue team! They were so happy!

Chapter 10
Rescue From The Cave

DERBY AND HER FRIENDS were cheering! Derby's dad James yelled, "We're here to rescue you!" The rescue team told the parents, "They're really far down in the cave! Our only option is to throw down a rope ladder and get them to climb up one at a time." Derby was the first one to climb the rope ladder. However, she was scared of heights! She realized how far up from the ground she was and started to get scared! Scarlett and James reassured Derby and said, "Don't look down! Just focus on us!" Eventually, Derby was able to make it out of the cave. Derby's parents were ecstatic that she safely made it out of the cave. Next, it was Peter's turn, he quickly climbed the ladder because he wasn't afraid of heights. Peter's parents gave him a big hug once he made it out of the cave. Byran was the last to climb the rope ladder. When he was about halfway up, the rope ladder came loose and started to sway side to side! The rescue team yelled, "Hold on!", as they tried to secure the ladder. Derby yelled down to Byran, "Don't worry, they are going to get you up safely!" Eventually the rescue team was able to secure the rope ladder, and Byran finished his climb to safety! All of the parents were relieved that Derby and her friends were safe. However, they were confused and furious as to how they ended up in a lifeboat, nevermind a cave! Derby explained to her parents how they got there. "Someone had put food into the lifeboat and we wanted to investigate. Once we got into the lifeboat, Sayer cut the ropes causing us to drift out to sea! We eventually crashed onto an island and decided to walk to a lighthouse where we met Owen the lighthouse keeper. We helped Owen, the lighthouse keeper, fix the communication equipment to radio in for help." Derby went on to say, "While we were on the island we met someone who introduced herself as an archeologist. She told us, if we helped her find a hidden treasure, she would give us a ride on her helicopter back to the cruise ship. So we agreed to help her find the treasure. The search involved going into this cave, going through traps, and solving puzzles! When we solved the last puzzle and got the treasure, the archaeologist trapped us under a net. It turned out that everything was a setup because once she had her treasure, she left us in the cave! We later found out that the person who cut the ropes of the lifeboat was actually her assistant. He was also the person flying the helicopter!" Derby and her friends' parents were in disbelief after hearing her story! Derby said, "I know how ridiculous this sounds, but we are telling the truth!" Derby and her friends' parents said, "That's impossible! There is no one else on this island!" Just then, Derby saw Owen the lighthouse keeper coming towards them. Derby and her friends' parents asked the man, "Who are you?" That's when Derby said, "this is Owen, the lighthouse keeper that I was telling you about!" The parents were in shock and started to believe the story that Derby was telling them. The lighthouse keeper told the parents and the rescue team, "I am the one who radioed you for help, and that's all! Thanks to your kids for helping me fix the communication equipment." The parents thanked Owen the lighthouse keeper for radioing in for help and keeping their kids safe. The rescue team told everyone, "We're going to give everyone a ride on the rescue boat back to the cruise ship." So, everyone got onto the rescue boat and took off towards the cruise ship.

Chapter 11
Saying Goodbye

EVERYONE ARRIVED SAFELY back at the cruise ship. They thanked the rescue team for helping with the search and rescue! Then, Captain Gary greeted Derby and her parents and told them that he was glad that they were all safe! Sadly, the cruise was almost over, and he was preparing to head back to the port the next day. Derby was disappointed by the news and said, "It's almost over?!" James said, "I'm afraid so." Peter and Bryan said to Derby, "Why don't we have one last fun day on the boat before heading home?" So, Derby and her friends headed back to the arcade to try their luck at some games. Derby and her friends saw a boxing game that they hadn't noticed before, so they decided to try it out. Derby and Peter decided to try it out first, while Bryan returned to the racing car game to beat his high score. After Bryan beat his high score in the racing game he decided to try out the boxing game while Derby and Peter played air hockey. Derby was confident that she was going to beat Peter. She had previously won against Bryan. Derby and Peter were tied 9-9 with only one goal left to score in the air hockey game. Derby looked away for one second and Peter scored and won the game! Peter was wondering why Derby had looked away, and noticed that she was looking at the TV in the arcade. Derby was distracted by a news report about a new discovery made by an archaeologist. The broadcaster went on to say that the archaeologist was unveiling her discovery at the Springshore Heights museum in two days. Derby, Peter, and Bryan were really upset by the news. Then, the parents came to the arcade to check in on the kids and noticed that Derby was watching the news broadcast. James and Scarlett were wondering what was going on. Derby explained that this was the archaeologist that trapped them in the cave! James and Scarlett told Derby that they would get home as fast as they could so they could go to the museum and explain what happened! However, Peter and Bryan's family didn't live in Springshore Heights. They told Derby and her parents to make sure that they go to the museum and tell the museum curator what happened back on the island. Then, they all decided to go to dinner together to try and unwind. They had to forget about what had happened until they got home and were able to fix the situation. They were all out for dinner together, one last time. This time Derby, Peter and Bryan decided to order hamburgers, while the parents ordered fish and chips for dinner. After finishing dinner, everyone headed back up to their rooms to pack their suitcases before going to bed. Early the next morning, the ship returned to the port and everyone headed off the ship. Gary the captain said to the passengers as they were disembarking, "Thanks for joining us on our cruise! We hope that you had a great time, and we are looking forward to seeing you again soon!" As Derby and her parents were getting off the ship, Peter, Bryan and their parents came over to say goodbye. Peter and Bryan said to Derby, "We had a good time, and we will keep in touch! We plan to send you some letters in the mail!" Derby said, "I had a good time too, and I will also send you both letters in the mail." James and Scarlett told Peter's parents Janice and Carl, and also Byran's parents Judy and Bradly, that they had a good time visiting on the cruise ship, and that they would also like to keep in touch. Then everyone parted ways.

Chapter 12
Getting To The Airport And Heading Home

DERBY AND HER PARENTS called a taxi to get a ride back to the airport. When the taxi driver arrived, sure enough, it was the same taxi driver as before! Jordan the taxi driver said to James, Scarlett, and Derby, "Nice to see you all again! Hop right in!" Once inside the taxi, Derby waved goodbye to the cruise ship before heading straight to the airport. When Derby and her family arrived at the airport, Jordan the taxi driver said again, "That will be $20 for the ride." So James paid Jordan the taxi driver $20, plus a tip for being so nice. Derby and her family headed into the airport and back through security. Derby was the first to go through security and have her bag checked. Once again the security guard was stunned by Derby's detective collection. Derby noticed the security guard was in disbelief and decided to tell him about her adventures. "I am currently working on a case involving an archaeologist and her assistant who tricked us into helping her find a hidden treasure! She had her assistant trick me and my friends into a lifeboat! Then he cut the ropes, causing us to drop into the ocean and then crash onto an island! She was on the island and she pretended to offer us a ride off the island if we helped her find a hidden treasure! Once the treasure was found, she abandoned us on the island and left us in a cave!" The security guard was shocked by Derby's story and asked her parents, "What's going on here?" James and Scarlett said, "I know! It was a scary situation! Right now we are on our way back home to go to the museum where the archaeologist is speaking about the treasure, and taking credit for finding it! Our plan is to tell the museum curator, Mr.Lee, what happened." After explaining the situation to the security guard, Derby and her parents finished heading through security and boarded the plane. Derby and her parents took their seats on the airplane, and once again, Jennifer the flight attendant offered her a drink and a cookie. Derby thanked Jenniffer for the food. Once Derby and her parents were settled into their seats, Mark the pilot came over the intercom and said, "Hello everyone, I am your captain and my name is Mark. We are about to take off so please make sure that you are buckled in." Then, slowly, the plane taxied towards the runway ready to take off into the sky. Once Derby and her family landed back in Springshore heights, they got off the plane, grabbed their luggage, walked to their car, and drove back home. When Derby and her parents arrived home, they unpacked their suitcases before having supper and heading to bed for a much needed rest. The next morning, Derby woke up and went downstairs. She saw her parents watching the TV. Apparently, the archaeologist was about to speak at the Springshore heights museum. Derby, James and Scarlett decided to go to the Springshore heights museum and tell Mr.Lee what happened. Quickly, Derby and her parents got in their car and drove to the museum.

Chapter 13
Confronting The Archaeologist

BACK AT THE MUSEUM, Kaitlyn the archaeologist had started her speech. She said that she had made a fantastic discovery that she wanted to show the world. So, Kaityln removed the blanket covering the diamond and said, "Behold! The lost treasure of lighthouse island!" Mr. Lee and the rest of the audience were very impressed by her discovery. However, Mr. Lee was curious how the archaeologist found the treasure, and asked, "How did you find the lost treasure?" Kaitlyn the archeologist said, "With the help of my assistant, Sayer, we were able to find the treasure pretty easily!" Just then, Derby and her parents arrived at the museum and went inside to find Mr.Lee. Once inside, Mr.Lee saw Derby and said, "Derby! It's nice to see you again!" Then Kaitlyn the archaeologist proclaimed loudly, "How did you escape off the island?!" Mr. Lee was confused and said, "Wait! What is going on here?" Kaitlyn the archaeologist said, "It's nothing! Nothing is going on here!" Derby interrupted Kaityln the archaeologist and said, " My new friends and I helped you find the treasure and then you left us in a cave with no way out! You also tricked us into the lifeboat, which is completely wrong!" Mr.Lee was shocked and asked Kaitlyn the archaeologist, "Is this true?" To avoid answering the question, Kaitlyn the archaeologist ran and grabbed the treasure! Then she headed towards the door with her assistant Sayer! Mr.Lee yelled to the security guards, "Stop her and her assistant!" The security guards tried to stop Kaityln the archaeologist and her assistant Sayer from escaping the building. However, Kaitlyn the archeologist was able to make it out of the museum and to her car. Kaitlyn and her assistant Sayer got into their car and drove away! Derby and her parents, as well as Mr. Lee, got in their vehicles in hopes of stopping the archaeologist from getting away with the treasure! While driving, Mr. Lee phoned the police to inform them that someone had escaped with a valuable treasure! They had acquired the treasure illegally! Meanwhile, Kaitlyn the archaeologist and Sayer noticed that they were being closely followed by Derby and her parents, and Mr. Lee. Kaitlyn said to Sayer, "We must lose them!" Then they noticed that the police had joined in on the chase! The police had set up roadblocks in hopes of catching the thieves. The police used their microphone and yelled, "Surrender now! You are under arrest!" Kaitlyn the archaeologist, and her assistant, had no choice but to pull over and start running on foot in hopes of evading the police! Kaitlyn and Sayer decided to take a quick turn down an alleyway! Derby and her parents, as well as Mr. Lee saw her go down the alleyway and decided to confront her! Kaitlyn and her assistant Sayer had to surrender at this point! They were put in handcuffs by the police, and taken to the police car. Mr. Lee grabbed the treasure and said, "Let's get this back to the museum!" Derby and her

DETECTIVE DERBY PRIVATE EYE AND THE MYSTERY OF LIGHTHOUSE ISLAND

parents headed back to the museum with Mr. Lee. Once back at the museum, Mr. Lee told Derby, "I am glad that you came forward and told me what happened. Otherwise I would have never known. You will make a really good detective one day!" This made Derby smile, and Derby thanked Mr.Lee for his help. Scarlett, James and Derby then decided to head home and enjoy the rest of their summer vacation.

Epilogue
The Presentation

WHAT HAPPENED AFTER summer break you ask? Well,Derby went on to do a presentation about her recent adventures as a detective. That included meeting some new friends on a cruise, getting tricked into a lifeboat, crashing onto an abandoned island, and getting tricked by an archaeologist to help find a treasure. Derby went on to say that while she was on the island looking for the treasure she had to avoid traps set by pirates, and solve puzzles to eventually find the lost treasure. When Derby and her friends found the treasure, the archaeologist decided to keep the treasure for herself and trap Derby and her friends in the cave. They were rescued from the cave by their parents and a rescue team. After being rescued and returning to the cruise ship, Derby said goodbye to her friends and went back home to expose everything the archaeologist had done. The confrontation with the archaeologist ended in a car chase together with the police. The archaeologist and her assistant were caught and put in a police car. As for Derby's friends, they still keep in touch by sending letters in the mail occasionally. The parents also keep in touch. Mr. Henry, as well as the rest of the class, was very impressed with Derby's presentation. Mr. Henry said to Derby, "It sounds like you had quite the adventure! What is going to be your next big mystery?" Derby said, "Well, I think I am going to wait until I am a little older before I solve my next mystery!"

The End

Don't miss out!

Visit the website below and you can sign up to receive emails whenever Isaiah Fransen publishes a new book. There's no charge and no obligation.

https://books2read.com/r/B-A-KMEP-UPVRC

BOOKS2READ

Connecting independent readers to independent writers.

Did you love *Detective Derby Private Eye And The Mystery Of Lighthouse Island*? Then you should read *Detective Derby Private Eye And The Birthday Heist*[1] by Isaiah Fransen!

Derby Is A Young Girl Who Wants Be A Detective When She Grows Up However When She Gets Invited To A Birthday Party And Valuable Item Goes Missing Her Dream Of Becoming A Detective Might Come Sooner Then She Thinks

---

1. https://books2read.com/u/b6lao6
2. https://books2read.com/u/b6lao6

Also by Isaiah Fransen

Detective Derby Private Eye
Detective Derby Private Eye And The Birthday Heist
Detective Derby Private Eye And The Mystery Of Lighthouse Island

Detective Jon
Detective Jon And The Missing Jewels
Detective Jon And The Missing Artifact
Detective Jon And The Hidden World
Detective Jon The All 3 Books In 1 Collection Small Book Edition
Detective Jon Books 1 To 3 Plus Before Jon The Complete Series And Prequel Bundle

Tasha The Last Princess Warrior
Tasha The Last Princess Warrior
Tasha The Last Princess Warrior Rise Of The Dark Princess Warrior

Tasha The Last Princess Warrior The Sorceress Of Power Before Tasha Plus Tasha The Last Princess Warrior Books 1 To 3 Prequel And The Complete Series Bundle

Standalone
Before Tasha
Before Jon

About the Author

Isaiah who has autism resides in the beautiful Okanagan Valley which is situated in the Southern part of British Columbia, Canada. Taking in the latest movies at the local theaters is one of his favorite pass times. His interest in solving mysteries has lead to his desire to write about them. His books is full of exciting plots and adventures. Playing video games keeps him busy the majority of his time but finds time in his sometimes hectic schedule to write and looks forward to publishing more of his work.

Milton Keynes UK
Ingram Content Group UK Ltd.
UKHW021103170924
448459UK00015B/810